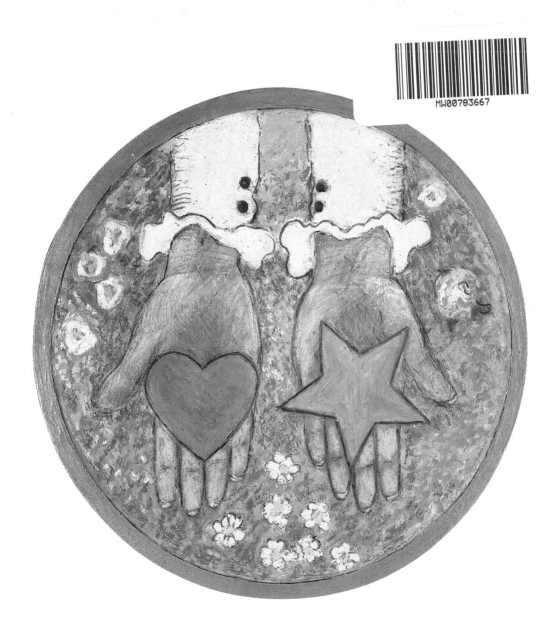

THE STARCLEANER REUNION

BY

Cooper Edens

Green Tiger Press

A Division of Laughing Elephant Books

3645 Interlake Avenue North

Seattle, Washington 98103

Second Edition / First Printing 2003 / Printed in China

ISBN 1-883211-74-3

And hearing the angel's
first words you begin
to reminisce...
and in your mind you
see pictures that show
more and more of the
world you knew at the
earliest of times.

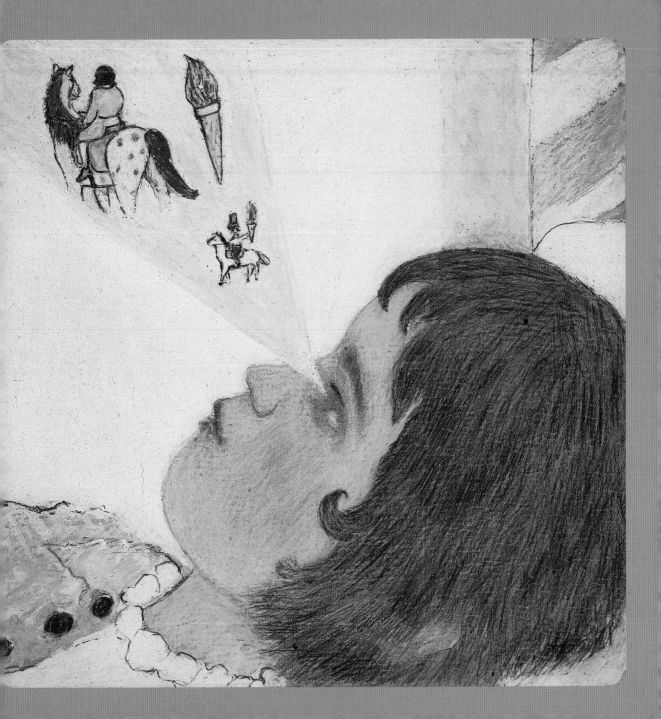

It was after silence was discovered and taught to speak, it was there in the eerie, unknown sounds of a place where it was too dark and each moment grew darker, that you first told the world about stars.

So on the plains of the dark sea's edge, we formed a circle and in the center you inscribed in the diary:

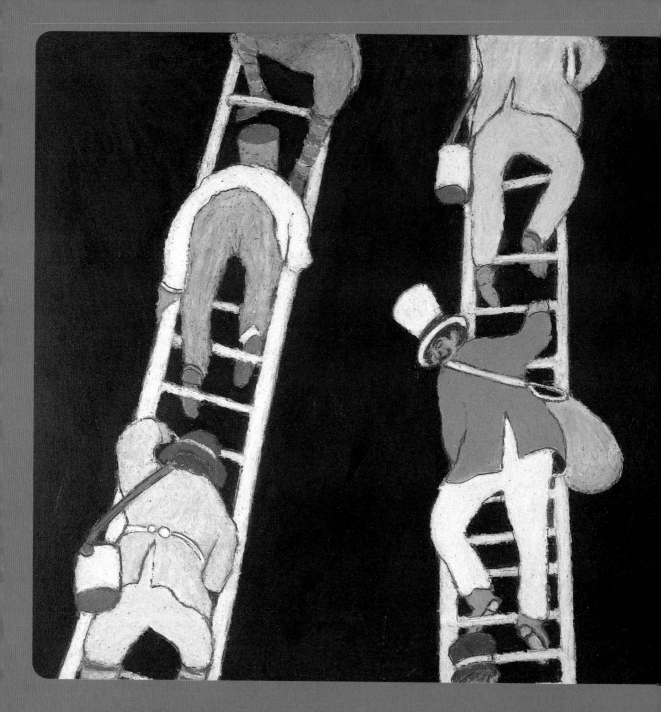

And when the finest,
sharpest points of all
the stars could be seen,
you asked for the angel
to name the light from
the closest one:

And when the first day turned slowly away, the new darkness flew over us and there was dancing in the great starlit tent around Earth.

Then suddenly the music stopped, catching us between steps! And onto our upturned faces, like rain, every star began to cry. The tears fell into the angel's great pointed hat until it overflowed.

Yet somehow with the world we stayed, and you appeared, the only one with any explanation for the strange behavior of the stars and the beginning of a remedy.

...we followed your direction, building a house that was large enough to hold every star. Then we spent long days collecting and bringing each one home.

When we got to the house
we polished the stars
even brighter, until they
shone like mirrors; and
then we tucked them,
warm and drowsy, into
cloud-like beds.

Then came the surprise. The house with all that happiness inside it burst. To hold it a bigger house appeared. Then an even bigger one! And a bigger one still!

And so it went on,
for what seemed forever.
The stars ought to have
been inside the biggest
house, but there was
always another, bigger one!

And soon the house
was so big it could not
be seen. It was then, in
a knowing way, that
you asked:

And search we did…
until at last we heard
the stars' tiny silver
voices. The stars' joy had
become so great, that they
had no place greater to
be. The stars became our
own hearts.

Every heart is part of the stars an

Goodnight everyone.

This book is typeset in Garamond
at Blue Lantern Studio.